Siggy and the Bullies

WRITTEN BY BLANCHE R. DUDLEY, Ed.D. • iLLUSTRATED BY LAWRENCE REYNOLDS

DOG EAR PUBLISHING

"Dedicated to Mama and Daddy whose unconditional love never faltered"

Praise For Siggy And The Bullies

Blanche Dudley brings a fresh perspective to combatting bullying with this heartwarming tale of triumph. Siggy may have physical challenges, but he more than rises to the challenge to escape two bullies after a wild chase! This beautifully illustrated story offers readers a powerful message: you don't have to face bullies alone. It's okay to tell. Adults can and will help. A must read for younger children and adults alike. Dudley invites us all to join Siggy's team!"

Laura Thieman, L.C.S.W., Clinical Social Work/Therapist

"Most children will experience or witness bullying at some point in their lives. This delightful story delivers a very simple, but profound, message to kids. Tell! It's important that trusted adults know what's going on! Good training!"

Dr. Anastasia Williams, M.D., Pediatrician

"Fun story, noteworthy lesson. Plain and simple, kids from kindergarten to high school need to know—and believe—that it's okay to tell when they or their friends are being bullied. It's never too early to start that conversation."

Archie Talley, M.S., Education, Former Professional Athlete, Motivational Speaker on "Self-Esteem" and "Bullying Is a Waste of Time"

"Bullying is a social problem that crosses all ethnic and economic class boundries and its negative impact can last throughout the life span. This courageous book offers help to stop bullying in its tracks before it is too late."

Theodore Fuller, Ph.D., LMFT Child Psychologist, Family Development Association, Inc.

First published by Dog Ear Publishing
4010 W. 86th Street, Ste H
Indianapolis, IN 46268
www.dogearpublishing.net

ISBN:978-1-4575-1993-2
Library of Congress Control Number: 2013913274

This book is a work of fiction. Places, events, and situations in this book are purely fictional and any resemblance to actual persons, living or dead, is coincidental.

Printed on acid free paper.
Printed in the United States of America

"Hurry, Siggy! Hurry!"

With the Bluejay twins right behind him, Siggy swerved toward his sisters, Pia and Gia.

e hopped
s fast as he
ould up the ladder
to the family's nest
the tall pine tree.

3

Swoosh!

Pia pulled Siggy inside,
tumbling him beak over tail feathers!

Bam! Gia slammed the door just as the Bluejays
banged into it.

4

"Whew!
That was close,"
wheezed Siggy.
"Vickie and Ickie
are always chasing me,
trying to peck my head
and pull my feathers!"

"Sometimes they pull my
feathers, too," said Pia.

"Those Bluejays are the
meanest birds I ever
saw," said Gia. "But
you're safe now. They
can't bully you here."

5

Siggy was a young mockingbird
whom Mama Sparrow had found abandoned
in the forest.

Now he lived with Mama
and had Pia and Gia for his sisters.

Siggy was different. He'd hatched with only one wing. He couldn't fly, but he could hop, moving easily along the ladder to and from their nest.

Best of all, though, he could mimic the sounds
of other birds in the forest,
which Pia and Gia thought was great.

Siggy just wished the Bluejays
wouldn't make so much fun of him.

"Wake up!" Mama Sparrow chirped the next morning. "Today we're making a welcome basket for the Hummingbirds who've just moved in next door.

Siggy, please find some nice red strawberries."

8

"Pia and Gia, please gather blueberries and a few sweet cherries. We'll make a lovely basket to attract lots of delicious fruit flies for our new neighbors."

"Yes, Mama," the chicks replied. And with a hop, hop, hop, they were up, up, up! After quick dips in the birdbath, they grabbed sacks and hurried outside.

9

Siggy hopped slowly
through the tall grass,
collecting strawberries.

His sack was almost full
when he saw his friend, Willie
Billie Woodpecker,
with one of the
new neighbors,
Hink Hummingbird.

"Hello," Siggy called.
"Where are you going?"

"We're running away from the Bluejay twins!" Willie Billie replied.

He and Hink fluttered down toward Siggy. "They're being mean to everyone today. You should watch out."

"Thanks," said Siggy. "Maybe if I'm very quiet, they won't see me."

Siggy continued gathering strawberries,
tiptoeing through the grass until ...

Oh, no! There was Vickie Bluejay
chasing Mrs. Duck and her ducklings.

"Quack! Quack! Get back!"
Mrs. Duck squawked at Vickie.

The ducks splashed into a nearby pond to escape.

Siggy closed his sack,
strapped it tightly around
his middle, and began
to back softly away.

"Croak! Croak!"

Oops! Siggy had stepped on a frog! He sped away as fast as he could.

But it was too late ...

The Bluejays had spotted him!

Caw! Caw! They zoomed toward him.

Siggy swerved.
Siggy sprinted.
Siggy rolled.
He zigged
and he zagged.
He hopped as fast
as he could.

But the bullies wouldn't give up. They dived and swooped and thrashed through the tall grass, getting closer and closer.

"Look at the little hop-along!" they taunted Siggy. "You'll never outrace us!"

Panting with fright, Siggy dove under a blackberry bush.

Vickie and Ickie waited nearby,
laughing and preening their glossy feathers.

Siggy peered at them through the brambles.
He couldn't fly, so how could he possibly escape?

Then he had an idea.

Siggy plucked up his courage and puffed up his chest.

In his best fake Mrs. Bluejay voice, Siggy cawed,
"Vickie! Ickie! Ickie! Vickie! Meet me at the honeysuckle patch on the far side of the meadow. Come
quickly! Caw! Caw!"

Siggy sounded exactly like Mrs. Bluejay.
But would the trick work?

Vickie and Ickie cocked their heads
this way and that way. "It's Mama! Let's go!"

They flew into the honeysuckle patch—smack-dab into huge, sticky spiderwebs!

Caw-ugh!
Caw-ugh!
They were stuck fast!

The Bluejays stomped and pushed and pulled. Honeysuckle flowers snapped and shot through the air like tiny yellow and white hailstones.

Vickie and Ickie stirred up such a ruckus that some of Siggy's friends who were playing nearby flew over to see what all the fuss was about.

When they saw the Bluejays caught in the gooey spiderwebs, they chirped and cheered.

"Ha! Ha! Heh! Heh! You can't bully us today!"

Siggy wiggled out from under
the blackberry bush
and hurried to join the other
birds fluttering around
the honeysuckle patch.

"Vickie and Ickie won't be chasing anyone for a while," he said. "Willie Billie, will you and Hink tell Mr. and Mrs. Bluejay where they can find the twins? I've got to take these strawberries home to Mama."

"Siggy, I was beginning to worry," Mama said when he got back. "What took you so long?"

"Vickie and Ickie were chasing me, and I had to hide until I could escape. I pretended to be Mrs. Bluejay and told them to meet her at the honeysuckle patch. They didn't know the patch was filled with sticky spiderwebs, so they got stuck! Willie Billie and Hink went to tell their parents what happened."

"You're our hero!" Gia cheered.

"Mama," Pia explained, "the Bluejay twins have been bullying Siggy and everybody—Gia and me, too—for a really long time. And Siggy finally outsmarted them!"

"You're a clever bird, Siggy, and I'm proud of you." Mama hugged Siggy. "I didn't know Vickie and Ickie were being so mean. Tomorrow, I'll talk to their parents. And I want the three of you to remember to tell me or another grown-up if bullies are ever hurting you or if you see them hurting someone else. Promise?"

"Yes! Yes! Yes!" The birds chimed in unison.

"Good,"
Mama nodded
as she turned to
find a nice ribbon for
the basket. "Now,
let's finish our gift
for the Hummingbirds
and then celebrate
with a fine dinner of
juicy worms
and hot-buttered
bugs. We can have
the leftover berries
for dessert."

"Yay!" cheered Siggy and his sisters.

"And maybe," Pia laughed, "we can get Siggy to do some impersonations!"

"Caw! Caw!" Siggy cackled with a wink and smile.

The End

LET'S TALK ABOUT iT!

What is bullying?

Siggy says bullying is doing something on purpose to make another person feel bad or afraid and doing it again and again, even if the person being hurt has asked the bully to stop.

What do you think? Does this sound like bullying?

Have you ever bullied anyone? Has anyone ever bullied you?

Why should you tell an adult?

Siggy would tell an adult because getting bullied hurts and makes the person being bullied feel very sad.

He knows that adults can talk to the bully or to the bully's parents or teacher about the bad behavior.

Siggy also believes adults can help him and his friends find a lot of other ways to stand up for themselves against a bully.

How about you? Why would you tell an adult?

Who are some of the adults you might tell if you or a friend were being bullied?

Siggy thinks he might tell:

Mama or Papa

Grandma or Grandpa

An aunt or an uncle

A teacher

The school principal

A troop leader

A school nurse

A coach

Do you think Siggy has a good list of adults to turn to for help?
Who are the adults you might tell about bullying?

More Tips from Siggy

Stand up for yourself. Tell the bully to stop.

Make a new friend.

Walk in a group with your friends. Don't stay alone.

Leave any place where you don't feel safe.
Tell an adult why.

Remember that you are loved.
Spend time with people you like and who like you.

BIOGRAPHIES

About the Author

Blanche R. Dudley, Ed.D., is the author of the new *Siggy* picture book series on anti-bullying for younger readers. Dr. Dudley earned a doctorate in education at West Virginia University and wrote a dissertation on enhancing the self-esteem of middle-school children. A retired educator and analyst, she now spends her free time writing and bird watching in her backyard where she finds inspiration for her picture book characters. The author lives in Reston, Virginia, with her husband, W. J. Dudley. You can visit Blanche and her storybook friends at www.blanchedudley.com. Also check out useful tips and resources for teachers, parents, and kids on her website.

About the Illustrator

Lawrence Reynolds specializes in the explosive collision of images, color, line, light, and shadow. Lawrence attended the Industrial Design program at the Center for Creative Studies: College of Art and Design in Detroit, Michigan. He later transferred into the Graphic Communication program and eventually majored in Art direction. He recalls that, "In art school, I stood out as *the art director who knew how to draw.*" After graduating in 1994, Lawrence began his career as an art director working on numerous national accounts for print and television. *Siggy and the Bullies* is his first children's book. Lawrence resides in Dallas, Texas. Visit the artist at www.vividfury.com.

CPSIA information can be obtained
at www.ICGtesting.com
Printed in the USA
BVHW01s2102080418
512516BV00014B/4/P